How the Loon lost her Voice

Anne Cameron

HARBOUR PUBLISHING CO. LTD.
1985

When I was growing up on Vancouver Island I met a woman who was a storyteller. She shared many stories with me, and later, gave me permission to share them with others.

This woman's name was KLOPINUM. In English her name means "Keeper of the River of Copper." It is to her this book is dedicated, and it is in the spirit of sharing, which she taught me, these stories are offered to all children. I hope they will enjoy them as much as I did.

Anne Cameron

Third Printing, 1987

Harbour Publishing Co. Ltd.
Box 219 Madeira Park B.C.
Canada V0N 2H0

There was a time when Loon was the most beautiful singer of all the birds on the island. She would float on the surface of the waves and pour her joy out in clear golden notes.

People would come to sit on the rocks and sand of the shore and listen to Loon sing her beautiful song. Other birds would gather in the branches of the trees, the animals would come from the forest, and while Loon sang, everybody felt happy. Even when it was raining and clouds covered the face of the sun, Loon would sing, and her song would warm the hearts of those who heard. Even the whales who live in the sea would surface and leap into the air, outlined against the sky, responding joyously to the beautiful song of the Loon.

Then tragedy came to the island. Evil spirits came from a place nobody knew, and they stole the daylight.

Shadows lay across the land. The trees lost their leaves. The berry bushes withered. The grass stopped growing. There was no food for the animals of the forest, or for the people.

The world grew cold and began to die.

All the people met together and began to pray. The drums beat, the dancers danced, the singers sang, and the holy people tried all the magic they knew.

But the world grew colder, the shadows darker, and the people despaired.

The animals met together to try to find a way to save the world.

"They have hidden the daylight," Raven said. "They have daylight locked in a box. They have cast a magic spell. There is a wall of ice encircling them and the box in which daylight is trapped."

"Then we must find a way to get the box, open it, and free the light," the Osprey said.

"We don't even know where the box is," Weasel said. "It could be anywhere at all behind that wall of ice."

Osprey nodded, and before anyone knew what she was going to do, she flew up, up, up, higher and higher, following the wall of ice up toward the sky.

Even Osprey was starting to get tired before she got to the top of the wall of ice. She looked over the top, her sharp eyes peering through the shadows and the darkness.

Finally, she saw a large, carved cedar box tightly tied shut with lengths of cedar bark.

Osprey flew to a point directly above the carved box then bent her wings, arched her back, and dove. Down, down, down, she plunged, but the evil spirits saw her coming and sent howling icy winds to blow Osprey back up into the sky.

Osprey tried time and time again, but she could not get close enough to the box to grasp it with her powerful claws. In the end, she was just too tired to try anymore, and she came back to where the animals were waiting, her feathers tinged with frost.

"I'm sorry," Osprey gasped, "I'm very sorry."

"Well," Raven said, "it's quite obvious we won't get in by the top."

"I'll get in," said the Deer confidently. "It's only a wall of ice. It isn't as if it were a wall of rock. I have very large, very strong antlers and I have very strong legs and shoulders. I'll just put my head down and bash a hole through the magic wall, then the rest of you can rush in, grab the box, and rush back out again. It will be easy."

"I don't think so," Raven said quietly. "I have never found force or violence to be the right way to get anything done." But nobody was listening. They were all cheering for the Deer.

Deer put his head down, bunched up his shoulder, and charged. Finally, his poor sore head could take no more and Deer came back to the group, looking quite ill. His proud antlers were broken completely off, his head bleeding and pained.

"Lie down here," Raven said, "I'll make a poultice for your sore head."

"**W**ell, then," rumbled the Bear, "It's obvious to me it's not the wall we have to defeat, it's the evil spirits who put it up. I'm going to go over there and challenge them to a wrestling match, for surely I am the finest wrestler in all the forest."

"I have my doubts about this," Raven said.

"Don't be silly," Bear bragged. "I'll just grab 'em and shake 'em and beat 'em, one by one, and when they've all been beaten, the magic wall will come down and everything will be fine. Just fine."

Bear lumbered toward the evil spirits roaring and beating his chest. He stomped his feet and threw rocks and sticks. He yelled insults and challenged the evil ones to a wrestling match.

The evil spirits turned, looked toward the bear, looked at each other, and shrugged. Then one of them crooked a magical finger and the bear was lifted, dropped, rolled,shaken, thumped, banged and pounded all over the ground.

When Bear finally got back down to his friends he was so exhausted he just lay down and fell into a deep sleep. Bear had been beaten!

"This will never do, you know," Loon said quietly. "I know," Raven answered, "but what are you going to do with ears that won't listen? Violence never solved anything."

"I have an idea," said Loon. "I'm very small, and I'm very black. and it is very dark. So the chances of my being seen are quite slim."

"And you, " Loon smiled at Mole, "you have beautiful big front paws, exactly what one needs to dig."

"Yes," said Mole, "I'm very lucky. But you must understand, I don't see very much. You'll have to lead me to wherever it is you want me to dig."

So Loon took Mole by the hand and led her to the wall of ice and cold that stood around the box in which daylight was locked.

"Thank you," Mole whispered. Then she lowered her head and began to dig in the frozen earth with her huge front paws, slowly, doggedly and very quietly.

18

When the hole was big enough to allow little Loon to crawl under the wall, Mole moved aside. Loon slithered under the wall and crept carefully toward the spot Osprey had indicated.

It was difficult for Loon to move quietly. Her feet were designed to paddle in water, not to walk on land. Her body was made to float and fly, not to creep over uneven ground in darkness.

But Loon managed!

When she was next to the large cedar box, she used her beak to untie the knots in the braided cedar rope, then she flung open the lid and reached for the daylight.

Loon has a white neck ring and when the daylight glittered on it the evil spirits saw her. They grabbed her by the neck swung her round in circles, and threw her back over the top of the wall of ice and cold.

Poor little Loon.

Poor brave little Loon.

She was thrown up, up, up higher than she had ever been before in her life, and then, dazed and only half alive, she fell down, down, down, landing in a heap on the ground with her poor neck stretched so long and thin her own friends could hardly recognize her.

When she tried to sing, only a sad noise came from her poor ruined vocal cords.

"This is terrible!" Raven exploded. "This is just terrible."

Raven hadn't been too upset when Deer lost his horns. She hadn't been upset at all—in fact she thought it was rather funny—when Bear lost the wrestling match. But to treat a little black bird so badly was something else altogether.

"This," said Raven "is not to be endured!" And Raven started off to where poor Mole was waiting beside the hole she had dug.

Raven moved much more perkily than poor Loon had been able to. She hopped and skipped over to the hole, slid through easily, and hurried to where daylight was laying in the half-open box.

Raven put her big wing over the top of the box and the little glimmer of light that had betrayed Loon was hidden. Working in total darkness, Raven scooped daylight from the box and tucked it under her wing. And because Raven is black all over, even her feet, even her beak, even her eyes, there was nothing to see in the darkness at all, and she had no trouble racing back to the hole under the wall of ice.

"Come on," said Raven, taking Mole by the hand.

"Thank you, " Mole smiled, gladly following Raven away from the cold.

When they got to where their friends
were waiting, she flung wide her wings and
RAVEN FREED THE DAYLIGHT!

The wall of ice began to melt. The icicles that
had formed on the bare branches began to drip
and shrink.

Daylight warmed the seeds waiting in the frozen earth
and they began to sprout and grow. Leaves budded
on the branches, and all of creation celebrated the
return of warmth and light.

"Oh!" squeaked Mole, "I can feel the warmth on my
skin." I am so grateful! Thank you, thank you all
very much!"

"We could never have done it without you, brave
Mole," Osprey said, flying up high to dance and sing
happily in the bright blue sky.

"Sing, dear Loon," the Mole asked, "Please sing a song of happiness for us all."

But when Loon opened her mouth to sing, they all realized what a terrible price she had paid in her attempt to free the daylight.

The only sound that came out was a sad, lonely call that made those who heard it think of all they once had, but lost.

"Oh, dear," said Mole, and a tear slid down her face.

"Don't cry, Mole," Loon said bravely, "perhaps my singing voice is gone, but it was worth it to bring back this warm sunshine and these beautifully scented blossoms. I don't mind."

As Loon said these words, there was sadness in her voice and a lump in her throat beneath her white neck rings.

"I really don't mind at all. It was worth it."

All of the animals were changed by their mighty struggle to free the daylight and to this day the Deer loses his antlers each fall, the bear rests from his labours by sleeping for long months, and the Raven loves bright shiny things.

And to this day also, every evening as the sun begins to set and dark of night begins, the Loon is reminded of the time she lost her singing voice, and her sad cry echoes across the water.